5/08

Spelling Bee

Pam Scheunemann

Illustrated by C. A. Nobens

Consulting Editor, Diane Craig, M.A./Reading Specialist

ABDO
Publishing Company

Published by ABDO Publishing Company, 4940 Viking Drive, Edina, Minnesota 55435.

Printed in the United States.

Credits
Edited by: Pam Price
Curriculum Coordinator: Nancy Tuminelly
Cover and Interior Design and Production: Mighty Media
Photo Credits: AbleStock, Creatas, Digital Vision, Steve Hopkin/Getty Images, John Foxx, ShutterStock

Library of Congress Cataloging-in-Publication Data

Scheunemann, Pam, 1955-
    Spelling bee / Pam Scheunemann; illustrated by Cheryl Ann Nobens.
       p. cm. -- (Fact & fiction. Critter chronicles)
    Summary: Bitsy the bee studies hard in hopes of winning the big spelling bee. Alternating pages provide facts about honeybees.
    ISBN 10 1-59928-472-3 (hardcover)
    ISBN 10 1-59928-473-1 (paperback)

    ISBN 13 978-1-59928-472-9 (hardcover)
    ISBN 13 978-1-59928-473-6 (paperback)
    [1. Spelling bees--Fiction. 2. Honeybee--Fiction. 3. Bees--Fiction. 4. Flowers--Fiction.] I. Nobens, C. A., ill.
 II. Title. III. Series.

    PZ7.S34424Spe 2007
    [E]--dc22

                                                                                2006005705

SandCastle Level: Fluent

SandCastle™ books are created by a professional team of educators, reading specialists, and content developers around five essential components—phonemic awareness, phonics, vocabulary, text comprehension, and fluency—to assist young readers as they develop reading skills and strategies and increase their general knowledge. All books are written, reviewed, and leveled for guided reading, early reading intervention, and Accelerated Reader® programs for use in shared, guided, and independent reading and writing activities to support a balanced approach to literacy instruction. The SandCastle™ series has four levels that correspond to early literacy development. The levels help teachers and parents select appropriate books for young readers.

Emerging Readers
(no flags)

Beginning Readers
(1 flag)

Transitional Readers
(2 flags)

Fluent Readers
(3 flags)

These levels are meant only as a guide. All levels are subject to change.

FACT & FICTION

This series provides early fluent readers the opportunity to develop reading comprehension strategies and increase fluency. These books are appropriate for guided, shared, and independent reading.

FACT The left-hand pages incorporate realistic photographs to enhance readers' understanding of informational text.

FICTION The right-hand pages engage readers with an entertaining, narrative story that is supported by whimsical illustrations.

The Fact and Fiction pages can be read separately to improve comprehension through questioning, predicting, making inferences, and summarizing. They can also be read side-by-side, in spreads, which encourages students to explore and examine different writing styles.

FACT OR FICTION? This fun quiz helps reinforce students' understanding of what is real and not real.

SPEED READ The text-only version of each section includes word-count rulers for fluency practice and assessment.

GLOSSARY Higher-level vocabulary and concepts are defined in the glossary.

SandCastle™ would like to hear from you.

Tell us your stories about reading this book. What was your favorite page? Was there something hard that you needed help with? Share the ups and downs of learning to read. To get posted on the ABDO Publishing Company Web site, send us an e-mail at:

sandcastle@abdopublishing.com

Honeybees live in groups called colonies. Each colony of bees has its own hive, or nest.

During summer vacation, Bitsy and her sister, Eva, work at their mom's shop, The Bee Hive. "Mom," Bitsy exclaims, "Eva won such a big trophy at the Flower Spelling Bee! I'd like to win one too!"

The hive is filled with wax honeycombs.
Bees make the large honeycombs one cell
at a time.

"Well," her mom says, "Eva can help you practice spelling while you collect pollen and nectar."

Honeybees have compound eyes made up of thousands of tiny lenses.

Bitsy is so excited! She wakes Eva early the next morning and buzzes around her until they reach the meadow. She sees so many different kinds of flowers. "I'll never learn to spell the names of all these flowers!" Bitsy says with dismay.

Honeybees must gather nectar from two million flowers to make a pound of honey.

Eva buzzes
down to a
sunflower
to gather
nectar as she tells
Bitsy, "It'll be easy. The
trick is to learn one word at a time
until you are sure you know it."

Bees collect pollen from flowers. Most honeybees eat a mixture of honey and pollen called bee bread.

Each day they break for a honey sandwich. Eva points at a daisy and asks, "Can you spell the name of that flower?"

Bitsy replies, "Daisy, d-a-i-s-y. Daisy!"

"Good work!" Eva exclaims.

Honeybees flap their wings up to 12,000 times a minute. This flapping helps dry the nectar and makes the buzzing sound we associate with bees.

At the end of the summer,
The Bee Hive is buzzing with
activity. "Clover, c-l-o-v-e-r. Clover,"
Bitsy says as she labels each jar.
"I think I've got it! I can't wait until
the spelling bee. It's only a week away!"

15

The word *bee* describes a busy gathering of people who come together for a special purpose, such as a spelling bee or a sewing bee.

On the day of the spelling bee, Bitsy watches
nervously while the other bees are spelling.
Angel makes it pretty far but misspells
snapdragon. It's down to Buzzby and Bitsy.

Bees are attracted to flowers that have bright colors and sweet scents.

The queen bee asks them to spell *marigold*. Buzzby misses by one letter. Bitsy thinks hard and says, "Marigold, m-a-r-i-g-o-l-d. Marigold." Eva and Mom cheer as Bitsy wins the big, shiny trophy!

FACT or FiCTioN?

Read each statement below. Then decide whether it's from the FACT section or the FiCTioN section!

1. Bees work in shops.

2. Honeybees have compound eyes.

3. Honeybees can flap their wings 12,000 times per minute.

4. Bees win trophies.

ANSWERS
1. fiction 2. fact 3. fact 4. fiction

Honeybees live in groups called colonies. Each 7
colony of bees has its own hive, or nest. 16

The hive is filled with wax honeycombs. Bees make 25
the large honeycombs one cell at a time. 33

Honeybees have compound eyes made up of 40
thousands of tiny lenses. 44

Honeybees must gather nectar from two million 51
flowers to make a pound of honey. 58

Bees collect pollen from flowers. Most honeybees 65
eat a mixture of honey and pollen called bee bread. 75

Honeybees flap their wings up to 12,000 times a 84
minute. This flapping helps dry the nectar and makes 93
the buzzing sound we associate with bees. 100

The word *bee* describes a busy gathering of people 109
who come together for a special purpose, such as a 119
spelling bee or a sewing bee. 125

Bees are attracted to flowers that have bright colors 134
and sweet scents. 137

During summer vacation, Bitsy and her sister,   7
Eva, work at their mom's shop, The Bee Hive.   16
"Mom," Bitsy exclaims, "Eva won such a big trophy   25
at the Flower Spelling Bee! I'd like to win one too!"   36

"Well," her mom says, "Eva can help you   44
practice spelling while you collect pollen and   51
nectar."   52

Bitsy is so excited! She wakes Eva early the   61
next morning and buzzes around her until they   69
reach the meadow. She sees so many different   77
kinds of flowers. "I'll never learn to spell the   86
names of all these flowers!" Bitsy says with dismay.   95

Eva buzzes down to a sunflower to gather   103
nectar as she tells Bitsy, "It'll be easy. The trick is   114
to learn one word at a time until you are sure   125
you know it."   128

Each day they break for a honey sandwich.   136
Eva points at a daisy and asks, "Can you spell   146
the name of that flower?"   151

Bitsy replies, "Daisy, d-a-i-s-y. Daisy!" 156

"Good work!" Eva exclaims. 160

At the end of the summer, The Bee Hive is 170
buzzing with activity. "Clover, c-l-o-v-e-r. Clover," 176
Bitsy says as she labels each jar. "I think I've got it! 188
I can't wait until the spelling bee. It's only a week 199
away!" 200

On the day of the spelling bee, Bitsy watches 209
nervously while the other bees are spelling. Angel 217
makes it pretty far but misspells *snapdragon*. It's 225
down to Buzzby and Bitsy. 230

The queen bee asks them to spell *marigold*. 238
Buzzby misses by one letter. Bitsy thinks hard and 247
says, "Marigold, m-a-r-i-g-o-l-d. Marigold." Eva and 253
Mom cheer as Bitsy wins the big, shiny trophy! 262

GLOSSARY

associate. to connect in the mind or imagination

dismay. a sudden loss of confidence due to fear or worry

gathering. a group of people meeting in one place

nectar. a sweet liquid found in flowers

pollen. the fine powder found in flowers

purpose. the reason for doing something

trophy. a prize given to the winner of a competition

wax. a yellow substance that bees make and then use to build honeycombs